Jane Austen
on
Love and Romance

S0-CFU-796

Copyright © 2011, 2016 by Constance Moore

All rights reserved. No part of this book may be reproduced in any manner without the express written consent of the publisher, except in the case of brief excerpts in critical reviews or articles. All inquiries should be addressed to Skyhorse Publishing, 307 West 36th Street, 11th Floor, New York, NY 10018.

Skyhorse Publishing books may be purchased in bulk at special discounts for sales promotion, corporate gifts, fund-raising, or educational purposes. Special editions can also be created to specifications. For details, contact the Special Sales Department, Skyhorse Publishing, 307 West 36th Street, 11th Floor, New York, NY 10018 or info@skyhorsepublishing.com.

Skyhorse® and Skyhorse Publishing® are registered trademarks of Skyhorse Publishing, Inc.®, a Delaware corporation.

Visit our website at www.skyhorsepublishing.com.

10 9 8 7 6 5 4 3 2 1

Library of Congress Cataloging-in-Publication Data is available on file.

Cover design by Laura Klynstra

Print ISBN: 978-1-5107-1205-8
Ebook ISBN: 978-1-62873-258-0

Printed in China

Jane Austen
on
Love and Romance

Jane Austen
Edited by Constance Moore

Skyhorse Publishing

CONTENTS

INTRODUCTION

Many of us have come across an aloof Mr Darcy or have fallen under the spell of a caddish Mr Wickham along the rocky path to true love, and it is these oh-so-true-to-life characters and her witty, gossipy, yet heartfelt observations that make Jane Austen's novels as pertinent today as when they were first written over two hundred years ago.

This collection of quotations, including extracts from letters to family and friends, accompanied by the illustrations of Hugh Thomson, C. E. Brock and H. M. Brock, will soothe those nerves and provide clarity and cultured explanations when it comes to matters of the heart.

LOVE

What a strange thing love is!

EMMA WOODHOUSE, *EMMA*

… nobody minds having what
is too good for them.

MANSFIELD PARK

If I could but know his heart,
everything would become easy.

MARIANNE DASHWOOD, *SENSE AND SENSIBILITY*

It is such a happiness when
good people get together
– and they always do.

MISS BATES, *EMMA*

She had been forced into prudence
in her youth, she learned romance
as she grew older.

PERSUASION

I suppose there may be a hundred
different ways of being in love.

EMMA WOODHOUSE, *EMMA*

FINDING YOUR SQUIRE

To you I shall say, as I have often said before, do not be in a hurry, the right man will come at last...

LETTER TO FANNY KNIGHT

If a woman is partial to a man, and
does not endeavour to conceal it,
he must find it out.

CHARLOTTE LUCAS, *PRIDE AND PREJUDICE*

But when a young lady is to be
a heroine, the perverseness of
forty surrounding families cannot
prevent her. Something must
and will happen to throw a
hero in her way.

NORTHANGER ABBEY

It is a truth universally acknowledged that a single man in possession of a good fortune, must be in want of a wife.

PRIDE AND PREJUDICE

There are certainly not so many
men of large fortune in the world,
as there are pretty women
to deserve them.

MANSFIELD PARK

There does seem to be a something
in the air of Hartfield which
gives love exactly the right
direction, and sends it into the
very channel where it
ought to flow.

EMMA WOODHOUSE, *EMMA*

The more I know of the world,
the more I am convinced that I
shall never see a man whom I can
really love. I require so much!
MARIANNE DASHWOOD, *SENSE AND SENSIBILITY*

A fortnight's acquaintance is
certainly very little. One cannot
know what a man really is by the
end of a fortnight. But if we do
not venture somebody else will.
MR BENNET, *PRIDE AND PREJUDICE*

I think him a very handsome young man, and his manners are precisely what I like and approve – so truly the gentleman, without the least conceit or puppyism.

AUGUSTA ELTON, *EMMA*

DRESS TO IMPRESS

Man only can be aware of
the insensibility of man
towards a new gown.

NORTHANGER ABBEY

Lady Catherine will not think the worse of you for being simply dressed. She likes to have the distinction of rank preserved.

WILLIAM COLLINS, *PRIDE AND PREJUDICE*

My hair was at least tidy, which was all my ambition.

LETTER TO CASSANDRA

A simple style of dress is so
infinitely preferable to finery... I
believe; few people seem to value
simplicity of dress, show and
finery are everything.

AUGUSTA ELTON, *EMMA*

You really must get
some flounces.

LETTER TO CASSANDRA

21

She had dressed with more than usual care, and prepared in the highest spirits for the conquest of all that remained unsubdued of his heart, trusting that it might be won in the course of the evening.

PRIDE AND PREJUDICE

He has but one fault, which time
will, I trust, entirely remove – it is
that his morning coat is a
great deal too light.

LETTER TO CASSANDRA

Considering how very handsome
she is, she appears to be little
occupied with it

GEORGE KNIGHTLEY, *EMMA*

Woman is fine for her own satisfaction alone. No man will admire her the more, no woman will like her the better for it. Neatness and fashion are enough for the former, and a something of shabbiness or impropriety will be most endearing to the latter.

NORTHANGER ABBEY

SHALL WE DANCE?

To be fond of dancing was a
certain step towards falling in love.

PRIDE AND PREJUDICE

I consider a country-dance as an emblem of marriage. Fidelity and complaisance are the principle duties of both; and those men who do not choose to dance or marry themselves, have no business with the partners or wives of their neighbours.

HENRY TILNEY, *NORTHANGER ABBEY*

There were twenty dances, and I danced them all, and without any fatigue.

LETTER TO CASSANDRA

Matrimony and dancing…
in both, man has the advantage
of choice, woman only the
power of refusal.

HENRY TILNEY, *NORTHANGER ABBEY*

27

If there had not been a Netherfield ball to prepare for and talk of, the younger Miss Bennets would have been in a very pitiable state.

PRIDE AND PREJUDICE

It may be possible to do without dancing entirely. Instances have been known of young people passing many, many months successively, without being at any ball of any description, and no material injury accrue either to body or mind.

EMMA

People that marry can never part, but must go and keep house together. People that dance only stand opposite each other in a long room for half an hour.

HENRY TILNEY, *NORTHANGER ABBEY*

I am much mistaken if there are not some among us to whom a ball would be rather a punishment than a pleasure.

CAROLINE BINGLEY, *PRIDE AND PREJUDICE*

THE GENTLE ART OF CONVERSATION

He smiled, looked handsome,
and said many pretty things.

PRIDE AND PREJUDICE

I could not be happy with a man whose taste did not in every point coincide with my own. He must enter into all my feelings; the same books, the same music must charm us both.

MARIANNE DASHWOOD, *SENSE AND SENSIBILITY*

One cannot be always laughing
at a man without now and then
stumbling on something witty.

ELIZABETH BENNET, *PRIDE AND PREJUDICE*

My idea of good company… is the
company of clever, well-informed
people who have a great
deal of conversation.

ANNE ELLIOT, *PERSUASION*

If I loved you less, I might be
able to talk about it more.

GEORGE KNIGHTLEY, *EMMA*

Laugh as much as you choose,
but you will not laugh me
out of my opinion.

JANE BENNET, *PRIDE AND PREJUDICE*

With men he can be rational and
unaffected, but when he has ladies
to please, every feature works.

GEORGE KNIGHTLEY, *EMMA*

34

How to Act

One fatal swoon has cost me my
life… Beware of swoons.

LAURA, *LOVE AND FREINDSHIP* [SIC]

… your arts and allurements may, in a moment of infatuation, have made him forget what he owes to himself and to all his family. You may have drawn him in.

LADY CATHERINE DE BOURGH, *PRIDE AND PREJUDICE*

There is no charm equal to tenderness of heart.

EMMA WOODHOUSE, *EMMA*

… you are conscious that your
figures appear to the greatest
advantage in walking.

FITZWILLIAM DARCY, *PRIDE AND PREJUDICE*

Good-humoured, unaffected girls, will not do for a man who has been used to sensible women. They are two distinct orders of being.

EDMUND BERTRAM, *MANSFIELD PARK*

[She] is one of those young ladies who seek to recommend themselves to the other sex by undervaluing their own, and with many men, I dare say, it succeeds. But, in my opinion, it is a paltry device, a very mean art.

CAROLINE BINGLEY, *PRIDE AND PREJUDICE*

There is safety in reserve, but no
attraction. One cannot love
a reserved person.

FRANK CHURCHILL, *EMMA*

I do not want people to be very
agreeable, as it saves me the
trouble of liking them a great deal.

LETTER TO CASSANDRA

… make the most of every half-hour in which she can command his attention. When she is secure of him, there will be leisure for falling in love as much as she chooses.

CHARLOTTE LUCAS, *PRIDE AND PREJUDICE*

We have all a better guide in ourselves, if we would attend to it, than any other person can be.

FANNY PRICE, *MANSFIELD PARK*

I think you are in a very grave
danger of making him as much
in love with you as ever.

ELIZABETH BENNET, *PRIDE AND PREJUDICE*

I could not excuse a man's having
more music than love – more ear
than eye – a more acute sensibility
to fine sounds than to my feelings.

EMMA WOODHOUSE, *EMMA*

You must not let your fancy
run away with you.

MRS GARDINER, *PRIDE AND PREJUDICE*

I was as civil to them as their bad
breath would allow me.

LETTER TO CASSANDRA

I am only resolved to act in a
manner which will constitute my
own happiness without reference
to you or any person so wholly
unconnected with me.

ELIZABETH BENNET, *PRIDE AND PREJUDICE*

A woman in love with one man
cannot flirt with another.

CATHERINE MORLAND, *NORTHANGER ABBEY*

COMPATIBILITY

Heaven forbid! – That would be
the greatest misfortune of all! – To
find a man agreeable whom one
is determined to hate!

ELIZABETH BENNET, *PRIDE AND PREJUDICE*

He perfectly agreed with her…
Emma felt herself so well
acquainted with him, that she
could hardly believe it to be
only their second meeting.

EMMA

A very desirable connection on
both sides, and I have not a doubt
of its taking place in time.

JOHN DASHWOOD, *SENSE AND SENSIBILITY*

… it is better to know as little as possible of the defects of the person with whom you are to pass your life.

CHARLOTTE LUCAS, *PRIDE AND PREJUDICE*

They said he was sensible, well-informed, and agreeable… his being her father's choice too, was so much in his disfavour.

LAURA, *LOVE AND FREINDSHIP*

To be sure, you knew no actual
good of me – but nobody thinks
of *that* when they fall in love.

ELIZABETH BENNET, *PRIDE AND PREJUDICE*

It would not be a bad thing for
her to be very much in love
with a proper object.

GEORGE KNIGHTLEY, *EMMA*

It would be an excellent match,
for he was rich, and she
was handsome.

SENSE AND SENSIBILITY

A large income is the best recipe
for happiness I ever heard of.

MARY CRAWFORD, *MANSFIELD PARK*

How little of permanent happiness
could belong to a couple who were
only brought together because
their passions were stronger
than their virtue.

PRIDE AND PREJUDICE

The mere habit of learning to love
is the thing; and a teachableness of
disposition in a young lady
is a great blessing.

HENRY TILNEY, *NORTHANGER ABBEY*

There could have been no two
hearts so open, no tastes so similar,
no feelings so in unison.

PERSUASION

51

He is a gentleman, and I am
a gentleman's daughter.
So far we are equal.
ELIZABETH BENNET, *PRIDE AND PREJUDICE*

He was exactly formed to
engage Marianne's heart.
SENSE AND SENSIBILITY

A fine young man and a lovely
young woman thrown together
in such a way, could hardly fail of
suggesting certain ideas to
the coldest heart and
the steadiest brain.

EMMA

He is also handsome… which a young man ought likewise to be, if he possibly can. His character is thereby complete.

ELIZABETH BENNET, *PRIDE AND PREJUDICE*

FALLING IN LOVE

The anxieties of common life
began soon to succeed to the
alarms of romance.

NORTHANGER ABBEY

I have come to feel for you a passionate admiration and regard, which despite my struggles, has overcome every rational objection.

FITZWILLIAM DARCY, *PRIDE AND PREJUDICE*

… where youth and diffidence are united, it requires uncommon steadiness of reason to resist the attraction of being called the most charming girl in the world.

NORTHANGER ABBEY

I am quite enough in love.

EMMA WOODHOUSE, *EMMA*

She had begun to think he
really loved her, and to fancy his
affection for her something
more than common.

MANSFIELD PARK

I cannot fix on the hour, or the spot, or the look or the words, which laid the foundation. It is too long ago. I was in the middle before I knew that I had begun.

FITZWILLIAM DARCY, *PRIDE AND PREJUDICE*

I must be in love; I should be the oddest creature in the world if I were not – for a few weeks at least.

EMMA WOODHOUSE, *EMMA*

The very first moment I
beheld him, my heart was
irrevocably gone.

LOVE AND FREINDSHIP

59

What could be more encouraging
to a man who had her
love in view?

MANSFIELD PARK

I remember I wore my yellow
gown, with my hair done up in
braids; and when I came into
the drawing-room, and John
introduced him, I thought I never
saw anybody so handsome before.

ISABELLA THORPE, *NORTHANGER ABBEY*

60

But that expression of 'violently in love' is so hackneyed, so doubtful, so indefinite, that it gives me very little idea. It is as often applied to feelings which arise from an half-hour's acquaintance, as to a real, strong attachment.

MRS GARDINER, *PRIDE AND PREJUDICE*

DECLARATIONS OF LOVE

My feelings will not be repressed.
You must allow me to tell you how
ardently I admire and love you.

FITZWILLIAM DARCY, *PRIDE AND PREJUDICE*

You pierce my soul. I am half agony, half hope… I have loved none but you.

CAPTAIN FREDERICK WENTWORTH, *PERSUASION*

I must therefore conclude that you are not serious in your rejection of me, I shall choose to attribute it to your wish of increasing my love by suspense, according to the usual practice of elegant females.

WILLIAM COLLINS, *PRIDE AND PREJUDICE*

She was the first object of his
love, but it was a love which
his stronger spirits, and bolder
temper, made it as natural for
him to express as to feel.

MANSFIELD PARK

I am really delighted with him;
he is full as handsome… and with
such an open, good-humoured
countenance that one cannot help
loving him at first sight.

ALICIA JOHNSON, *LADY SUSAN*

I could not think about you so
much without doting on you,
faults and all…

GEORGE KNIGHTLEY, *EMMA*

65

Oh! she is the most beautiful
creature I ever beheld!

CHARLES BINGLEY, *PRIDE AND PREJUDICE*

Very long has it possessed a charm
over my fancy; and, if I dared, I
would breathe my wishes that the
name might never change.

WILLIAM ELLIOT, *PERSUASION*

MEN IN LOVE

… his air as he walked by the house – the very sitting of his hat… all in proof of how much he was in love!

EMMA

67

Darcy had never been so bewitched by any woman as he was by her. He really believed, that were it not for the inferiority of her connections, he should be in some danger.

PRIDE AND PREJUDICE

I cannot think well of a man who sports with any woman's feelings; and there may often be a great deal more suffered than a stander-by can judge of.

FANNY PRICE, *MANSFIELD PARK*

I could not reason so
to a man in love.

GEORGE KNIGHTLEY, *EMMA*

That he should think it worth his
while to fancy himself in love
with her was a matter of
lively astonishment.

NORTHANGER ABBEY

A young man, such as you describe
Mr Bingley, so easily falls in love
with a pretty girl for a few weeks,
and when accident separates
them, so easily forgets her.

MRS GARDINER, *PRIDE AND PREJUDICE*

It would be mortifying to the
feelings of many ladies could
they be made to understand how
little the heart of man is affected
by what is costly or new in their
attire; how little it is biased by the
texture of their muslin.

NORTHANGER ABBEY

70

… he must be in love with you or
he would never have called on
us in this familiar way.

CHARLOTTE LUCAS, *PRIDE AND PREJUDICE*

71

She attracted him more than he liked… He wisely resolved to be particularly careful that no sign of admiration should *now* escape him.

PRIDE AND PREJUDICE

… men are much more philosophic on the subject of beauty than they are generally supposed; till they do fall in love with well-informed minds instead of handsome faces.

EMMA WOODHOUSE, *EMMA*

Had he married a more amiable woman, he might have been made still more respectable than he was: he might even have been made amiable himself.

SENSE AND SENSIBILITY

I have never yet found that the advice of a sister could prevent a young man's being in love if he chose it.

LADY SUSAN VERNON, *LADY SUSAN*

A man does not recover from such
devotion of the heart to such a
woman! He ought not;
he does not.

CAPTAIN FREDERICK WENTWORTH, *PERSUASION*

No man is offended by another man's admiration of the woman he loves; it is the woman only who can make it a torment.

HENRY TILNEY, *NORTHANGER ABBEY*

WOMEN IN LOVE

Next to being married, a girl likes
to be crossed a little in
love now and then.

MR BENNET, *PRIDE AND PREJUDICE*

This sensation of listlessness, weariness, stupidity, this disinclination to sit down and employ myself, this feeling of every thing's being dull and insipid about the house!
I must be in love.

EMMA WOODHOUSE, *EMMA*

I have no notion of loving people by halves; it is not my nature.

ISABELLA THORPE, *NORTHANGER ABBEY*

She had talked her into love; but,
alas! She was not so easily
to be talked out of it.

EMMA

… no young lady can be justified
in falling in love before the
gentleman's love is declared, it
must be very improper that a lady
should dream of a gentleman
before the gentleman is first
known to have dreamt of her.

NORTHANGER ABBEY

I must love him; and now that
I am satisfied on one point, the
one material point, I am sincerely
anxious for its all turning out well,
and ready to hope that it may.

ANNE WESTON, *EMMA*

A young woman in love always
looks – *like Patience on a
monument / Smiling at Grief.*

QUOTING WILLIAM SHAKESPEARE IN *NORTHANGER ABBEY*

79

She began now to comprehend
that he was exactly the man, who,
in disposition and talents,
would most suit her.

PRIDE AND PREJUDICE

A lady's imagination is very rapid;
it jumps from admiration to love,
from love to matrimony
in a moment.
FITZWILLIAM DARCY, *PRIDE AND PREJUDICE*

[She] was one of those, who,
having, once begun, would
be always in love.
EMMA

81

It is very often nothing but our
own vanity that deceives us.
Women fancy admiration means
more than it does.

JANE BENNET, *PRIDE AND PREJUDICE*

I do suspect that he is not really
necessary to my happiness. So
much the better. I certainly will
not persuade myself to feel
more than I do.

EMMA WOODHOUSE, *EMMA*

82

Upon my word, I never saw a
young woman so desperately
in love in my life!

MRS JENNINGS, *SENSE AND SENSIBILITY*

Till now that she was threatened
with its loss, Emma had never
known how much of her
happiness depended on being
first with Mr Knightley, first
in interest and affection.

EMMA

You are too sensible a girl…
to fall in love merely because
you are warned against it.

MRS GARDINER, *PRIDE AND PREJUDICE*

An Engagement

It is always incomprehensible to
a man that a woman should ever
refuse an offer of marriage. A man
always imagines a woman to be
ready for any body who asks her.

EMMA WOODHOUSE, *EMMA*

85

I would rather work for my
bread than marry him.

FREDERICA VERNON, *LADY SUSAN*

Seven years would be insufficient
to make some people acquainted
with each other, and seven days
are more than enough for others.

MARIANNE DASHWOOD, *SENSE AND SENSIBILITY*

We see every day that where there is affection, young people are seldom withheld by immediate want of fortune from entering into engagements with each other.

ELIZABETH BENNET, *PRIDE AND PREJUDICE*

If a woman *doubts* as to whether she should accept a man or not, she certainly ought to refuse him.

EMMA WOODHOUSE, *EMMA*

An engaged woman is always more agreeable than a disengaged. She is satisfied with herself. Her cares are over, and she feels that she may exert all her powers of pleasing without suspicion.

HENRY CRAWFORD, *MANSFIELD PARK*

If you go on refusing every offer of marriage, you will never get a husband at all.

MRS BENNET, *PRIDE AND PREJUDICE*

Yes, quite a proposal of marriage;
and a very good letter, at
least she thought so.

EMMA

When a young man… comes and makes love to a pretty girl, and promises marriage, he has no business to fly off from his word only because he grows poor, and a richer girl is ready to have him.

MRS JENNINGS, *SENSE AND SENSIBILITY*

What are you doing? Are you out of your senses to be accepting this man? Have you not always hated him?

MR BENNET, *PRIDE AND PREJUDICE*

A woman is not to marry a man
merely because she is asked.

EMMA WOODHOUSE, *EMMA*

… self-interest alone could induce
a woman to keep a man to an
engagement, of which she
seemed so thoroughly aware
that he was weary.

SENSE AND SENSIBILITY

MARRIAGE

Oh! The best nature in
the world – a wedding.

EMMA WOODHOUSE, *EMMA*

His temper might perhaps be a little soured by finding, like many others of his sex, that through some unaccountable bias in favour of beauty, he was the husband of a very silly woman.

SENSE AND SENSIBILITY

… do anything rather than marry without affection.

JANE BENNET, *PRIDE AND PREJUDICE*

He is rich, to be sure, and you may
have more fine clothes and fine
carriages than Jane. But will
they make you happy?

MR BENNET, *PRIDE AND PREJUDICE*

I would rather be a teacher at a school (and I can think of nothing worse) than marry a man I did not like.

EMMA, *THE WATSONS*

Oh! You will think very differently, when you are married.

CAPTAIN FREDERICK WENTWORTH, *PERSUASION*

Single women have a dreadful propensity for being poor. Which is one very strong argument in favour of matrimony.

LETTER TO FANNY KNIGHT

She must be attached to you, or she would not have married you.

ELINOR DASHWOOD, *SENSE AND SENSIBILITY*

Without thinking highly either of men or of matrimony, marriage had always been Charlotte Lucas's object; it was the only honourable provision for well-educated young women of small fortune.

PRIDE AND PREJUDICE

One may as well be single if the wedding is not to be in print.

LETTER TO CASSANDRA

In marriage, the man is supposed
to provide for the support of the
woman, the woman to make the
home agreeable to the man; he is to
purvey, and she is to smile.

HENRY TILNEY, *NORTHANGER ABBEY*

… a good man must feel, how wretched, and how unpardonable, how hopeless, and how wicked it was to marry without affection.

MANSFIELD PARK

When two young people take it into their heads to marry, they are pretty sure by perseverance to carry their point.

PERSUASION

99

I consider everybody as having a right to marry once in their lives for love, if they can.

LETTER TO CASSANDRA

In marriage especially… there is not one in a hundred of either sex who is not taken in when they marry… I consider that it is, of all transactions, the one in which people expect most from others, and are least honest themselves.

MARY CRAWFORD. *MANSFIELD PARK*

Did you ever hear the old song
'Going to One Wedding
Brings on Another'?

JOHN THORPE, *NORTHANGER ABBEY*

The whole subject of it was love – a marriage of love was to be described by the gentleman, and very little short of a declaration of love be made by the lady.

MANSFIELD PARK

Breaking Up

The visions of romance were over.

NORTHANGER ABBEY

He had ruined for a while every
hope of happiness for the most
affectionate, generous heart in the
world; and no one could say
how lasting an evil he
might have inflicted.

PRIDE AND PREJUDICE

I shall do very well again after a
little while – and then, it will be
a good thing over; for they say
everyone is in love once in their
lives, and I shall have been
let off easily.

EMMA WOODHOUSE, *EMMA*

We certainly do not forget you as
soon as you forget us.

CAPTAIN HARVILLE, *PERSUASION*

I had not known you a month
before I felt that you were the last
man in the world whom I could
ever be prevailed on to marry.

ELIZABETH BENNET, *PRIDE AND PREJUDICE*

I am glad I have done being
in love with him.

EMMA WOODHOUSE, *EMMA*

She was convinced that she could
have been happy with him; when
it was no longer likely that
they should meet.

PRIDE AND PREJUDICE

Friendship is certainly the finest
balm for the pangs of
disappointed love.

NORTHANGER ABBEY

It was gratitude; gratitude, not merely for having once loved her, but for loving her still well enough to forgive all the petulance and acrimony of her manner in rejecting him.

PRIDE AND PREJUDICE

Dare not say that man forgets sooner than woman, that his love has an earlier death.

CAPTAIN FREDERICK WENTWORTH, *PERSUASION*

If he is satisfied with only regretting me, when he might have obtained my affections and hand, I shall soon cease to regret him at all.

ELIZABETH BENNET, *PRIDE AND PREJUDICE*

The course of true love never did run smooth – A Hartfield edition of Shakespeare would have a long note on that passage.

EMMA WOODHOUSE, *EMMA*

I am now convinced… that I have
never been much in love; for had
I really experienced that pure
and elevating passion, I should at
present detest his very name, and
wish him all manner of evil.

ELIZABETH BENNET, *PRIDE AND PREJUDICE*

I have been always used to a very
small income, and could struggle
with any poverty for him; but I
love him too well to be the selfish
means of robbing him.

LUCY STEELE, *SENSE AND SENSIBILITY*

110

At length the day is come on
which I am to flirt my last
with Tom Lefroy, and when
you receive this it will be over.
My tears flow as I write at the
melancholy idea.

LETTER TO CASSANDRA

111

She told him that she did not
love him, could not love him,
was sure she never should love
him; that such a change was quite
impossible; that the subject was
most painful to her; that she must
entreat him never to mention it
again, to allow her to leave him at
once, and let it be considered as
concluded for ever.

MANSFIELD PARK

UNREQUITED LOVE

… there are very few of us who have heart enough to be really in love without encouragement.

CHARLOTTE LUCAS, *PRIDE AND PREJUDICE*

… he is so very much occupied by the idea of *not* being in love with her, that I should not wonder if it were to end in his being so at last.

ANNE WESTON, *EMMA*

My real purpose was to see you, and to judge, if I could, whether I might ever hope to make you love me.

FITZWILLIAM DARCY, *PRIDE AND PREJUDICE*

Nothing can compare to the
misery of being bound to one,
and preferring another.

LETTER TO FANNY KNIGHT

115

Never had she so honestly felt that
she could have loved him,
as now, when all love
must be in vain.

PRIDE AND PREJUDICE

I shall do very well again after a
little while – and then, it will be a
good thing over; for they say every
body is in love once in their lives,
and I shall have been let off easily.

EMMA WOODHOUSE, *EMMA*

All the privilege I claim for my own sex… is that of loving longest, when existence or when hope is gone.

ANNE ELLIOT, *PERSUASION*

I wonder who first discovered the efficacy of poetry in driving away love!

ELIZABETH BENNET, *PRIDE AND PREJUDICE*

I should like to see Emma in love,
and in some doubt of a return; it
would do her good.

GEORGE KNIGHTLEY, *EMMA*

There will be little rubs and
disappointments everywhere,
and we are all apt to expect too
much; but then, if one scheme of
happiness fails, human nature turns
to another; if the first calculation is
wrong, we make a second better:
we find comfort somewhere.

MRS GRANT, *MANSFIELD PARK*

I cannot help feeling for those
that are crossed in love.

ELIZABETH WATSON, *THE WATSONS*

There was a great deal of friendly
and compassionate attachment on
his side – but no love.

EMMA

It does not often happen that
the interference of friends
will persuade a young man of
independent fortune to think
no more of a girl whom he was
violently in love with only
a few days before.

ELIZABETH BENNET, *PRIDE AND PREJUDICE*

… to flatter and follow others,
without being flattered and
followed in turn, is but a state of
half enjoyment.

PERSUASION

There are such beings in the
world – perhaps one in a thousand
– as the creature you and I think
perfection: where grace and spirit
are united to worth… such a
person may not come in your way,
or, if he does, he may not be the
eldest son of a man of fortune.

LETTER TO FANNY KNIGHT

121

If it were love, it might be
simple, single, successless
love on her side alone.

EMMA

HAPPILY EVER AFTER

Happiness in marriage is
entirely a matter of chance.

CHARLOTTE LUCAS, *PRIDE AND PREJUDICE*

One man's ways may be as good as
another's, but we all like
our own best.

ANNE ELLIOT, *PERSUASION*

It is settled between us already,
that we are to be the happiest
couple in the world.

ELIZABETH BENNET, *PRIDE AND PREJUDICE*

… endeavour to give the other no
cause for wishing that
he or she had bestowed
themselves elsewhere.

HENRY TILNEY, *NORTHANGER ABBEY*

… she laughed heartily to think
that her husband could not get
rid of her… she did not care how
cross he was to her, as they
must live together.

SENSE AND SENSIBILITY

Risk anything rather
than her displeasure.

MR BENNET, *PRIDE AND PREJUDICE*

I wish as well as every body else to
be perfectly happy; but like
every body else, it must
be in my own way.

EDWARD FERRARS, *SENSE AND SENSIBILITY*

When two sympathetic hearts
meet in the marriage state,
matrimony may be
called a happy life.

MARY CRAWFORD, *MANSFIELD PARK*